THE HANUKKAH TRIKE

MICHELLE EDWARDS   Illustrated by **KATHRYN MITTER**

Albert Whitman & Company, Chicago, Illinois

Library of Congress Cataloging-in-Publication Data

Edwards, Michelle.
The Hanukkah trike / Michelle Edwards ; illustrated by Kathryn Mitter.
p. cm.
Summary: After falling off of the tricycle she just received as a Hanukkah gift, Gabi recalls the story
of the brave Maccabees and finds the courage to try again.
ISBN 978-0-8075-3126-6
[1. Hanukkah—Fiction. 2. Bicycles and bicycling—Fiction. 3. Jews—Fiction.] I. Mitter, Kathy, ill. II. Title.
PZ7.E262Han 2010   [E]—dc22   2010006247

The art is painted in acrylics on Bristol board.
The design is by Carol Gildar.

For more information about Albert Whitman & Company,
please visit our web site at www.albertwhitman.com.

To Natalie Blitt, the story fairy. In gratitude for granting my hopes and wishes.—M.E.

Gabi Greenberg loved Hanukkah. She loved to watch the sun go down. She loved to see the sky grow dark. When the stars appeared, she loved to light the menorah.

For tonight, the first night of Hanukkah, Gabi chose a red candle and a yellow one. Mama lit the red *shammash*, the helper candle, and gave it to Gabi. Gabi lit the yellow candle. She put the *shammash* in its special spot on the menorah.

"Two little candles burning brightly," she sang. She watched them flicker and glow. Then it was time for latkes!

Gabi helped Daddy grate the potatoes. Mama made the batter and fried the latkes golden and crisp. Gabi filled bowls with applesauce, jam, and sour cream.

"Yum," said Gabi. "I could eat a million. Yum. Yum."

When dinner was over, not a single latke was left. Mama found the dreidel. Gabi twirled it round and round.

"*Nun, gimel, hay, shin,*" said Daddy. Those were the Hebrew letters on the dreidel. "They mean 'a great miracle happened there.' That's the story of Hanukkah."

"Long, long ago in the ancient land of Israel," continued Daddy, "King Antiochus tried to stop the Jewish people from celebrating their holidays, speaking Hebrew, and praying to one God. He wanted everyone to be just like him. The Maccabees and their friends fought Antiochus and his big army."

"And they won!" shouted Gabi.

"Yes, and when they won," said Daddy, "they went to Jerusalem, to the holy Temple. It was dark, dirty, and messy. They lit the big seven-branched candelabra. And even though they were very tired, the Maccabees started to scour and scrub. They wanted the Temple to look special again. They worried that they had just enough oil to light the Temple that first night, but—"

"But it lasted for eight nights!" said Gabi. "It was a miracle."

"That's why we light candles on Hanukkah," said Daddy. "To remember the brave Maccabees and celebrate the miracle of the light that burned for eight nights."

"Happy Hanukkah, Gabi," said Mama. She was pushing something with a huge bow and three wheels.

"Yippee!" said Gabi. "A trike for me!" She sat on the big seat. She put her hands on the wide handlebars. She felt tall and important.

"I'm going to call it Hanukkah," she said.
"And I will ride it everywhere."

The very next day, Gabi put Blankie in Hanukkah's basket. She tried to scoot. But Hanukkah didn't move.

Gabi tried to pedal. Her feet slipped and slid.

"Brummm, brummm, brummm."

Gabi stood up. She pushed her feet down really hard. Hanukkah wobbled and tipped over.

"Owie!" cried Gabi. Mud and tiny pebbles covered her hand. Her tights tore. "Owie! Owie!!"

Gabi held Blankie as Mama kissed her better.
"I think Hanukkah's too dirty to ride," Gabi said.
She hugged Blankie tight.

"We could clean it like the Maccabees did," Mama told her. She got a bucket of warm water and two rags. Together, they sponged and wiped and swabbed. Soon Hanukkah looked new again.

"The Maccabees were brave," said Gabi.

"They were *very* brave," said Mama.

"Do you think the Maccabees were ever scared?" asked Gabi. She rubbed Hanukkah's clean seat.

"I bet they were scared," said Mama. "But they didn't give up."

"And they won," said Gabi. She sat down.

"That's why we celebrate Hanukkah," said Mama.

Gabi put Blankie back in the basket. She checked the hole in her tights. She put her feet on the pedals. They stayed right there. Then Mama gave a gentle push.

Slowly the wheels turned. Hanukkah moved a little bit.
Gabi pedaled harder. Hanukkah moved faster and faster.

"I did it! I did it! I did it!" Gabi shouted.
"I'm brave like the Maccabees!"
And Gabi and Hanukkah went speeding
down the sidewalk.